Emma The Bumble Bee

Emma The Bumble Bee

Written and Illustrated by Monica Dumont

To Emma, my little bumble bee
and all the other beautiful children in my life -D.S.J.A.

Emma the bumble bee had to go and collect pollen from the spring flowers for the first time.

She was a little bit worried that she would not know how to do it and that she might not find her way back home.

The other bumble bees told her not to worry, for bees always find their way.

As Emma set off alone on her journey, she soon found a beautiful field overflowing with flowers.

Excited, she approached a fuchsia-colored flower and wondered what she should do next.

Then she started to think about how unfair it was to be a bumble bee. She did not like that she had to go and collect pollen all by herself without anyone ever teaching her how.

She sat on one of the petals moping and feeling sorry for herself.

A long, long time passed and Emma fell asleep.

When she woke up, she noticed that she
was feeling much better. She stretched
and took a few deep breaths.

Suddenly she noticed how beautiful the colours of the flowers were and how pretty the dusty pollen on the flowers was.

With all of these good thoughts, she started to feel a very strong, warm feeling coming from just below her chest.

The feeling was so strong and wonderful, that it started to rise up into her heart and flow outwards, surrounding her.

Then she heard a voice say, "I believe you have found your inner power."

It was an older bumble bee who had been following her and watching after her from far away.

Little Emma smiled and followed her feelings. Trusting herself, she collected just the right amount of pollen to bring back home.

The older bumble bee accompanied her back home and when they arrived, all the other bumble bees greeted her with cheers and many, many, many hugs.

The End

Book Challenge:

Step 1: Ask a parent, guardian or an adult you like, to help you think of a time in which you trusted yourself and everything went well.

(If you cannot come up with something, ask your adult friend to share one of his or her experiences with you.)

Step 2: Now for the rest of the week, notice how you feel in different situations.

Step 3: If you realize that you are feeling uncertain, frustrated, afraid, angry or even sad because things seem a little bit difficult. (Like Emma the bumble bee) you too, can find your inner power!

Step 4: Find a private space like your room or a washroom. Then close your eyes, put one hand in the centre of your chest and raise your head. Now take a deep breath and exhale it slowly. Smile, open your eyes and notice how great you feel.

Step 5: Trust yourself.

Step 6: At the end of each day, ask your adult friend to help you write and discuss how you dealt with the situation and how doing your breathing exercise helped you.

Please note:
This exercise is meant to help parents bond with their child as well as to help their child develop new skills at dealing with everyday life. It is not meant to be used as a form of therapy.

My Exercise Log 1

My Exercise Log 2

_____
_____
_____
_____
_____
_____
_____
_____
_____
_____
_____
_____
_____

My Exercise Log 3

_____
_____
_____
_____
_____
_____
_____
_____
_____
_____
_____
_____

Colour me

CPSIA information can be obtained
at www.ICGtesting.com
Printed in the USA
BVHW020316150520
579736BV00010B/56